Clever Chameleon

Written and illustrated by
Ali Lodge

Barefoot Books
Celebrating Art and Story

In the jungle, one fine day,
The creatures all came out to play.
Parrot clicked his shiny beak,
"Let's play a game of hide-and-seek!"

"I want to count!" Elephant cried,
And everyone went off to hide.

"Five and four, and three, two, one...
Ready or not ... here I come!"

Leopard with her patterned fur
Stretched out on a branch to purr.
She blended with the jungle light
And that helped her stay out of sight.

Proud Giraffe, towering high,
Could almost reach right to the sky.
Her spotted coat, shaped like leaves,
Helped her to hide among the trees.

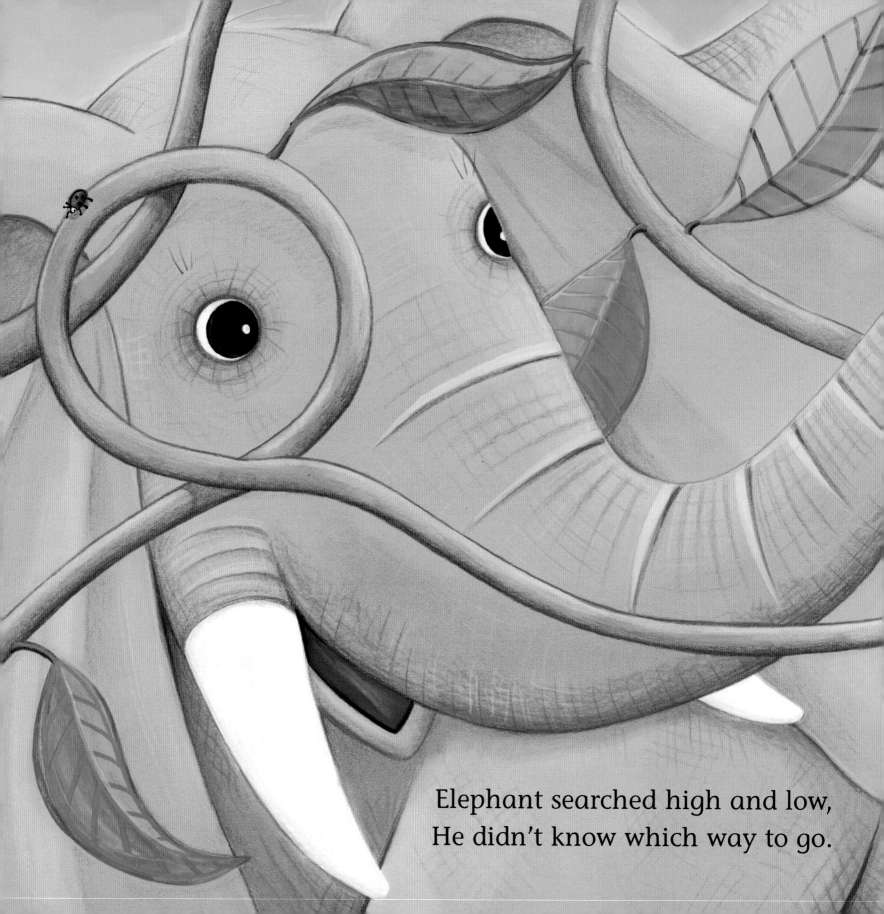

Elephant searched high and low,
He didn't know which way to go.

But suddenly, to his delight,
He spotted Parrot, small and bright!

Then a rustling from the grass
Disturbed the pair as they walked past.
Who goes there? Can you tell?
But Lion's coat concealed him well.

Elephant looked here and there,
Through the leaves and everywhere!
He saw some logs and gave a smile,
One log looked like Crocodile!

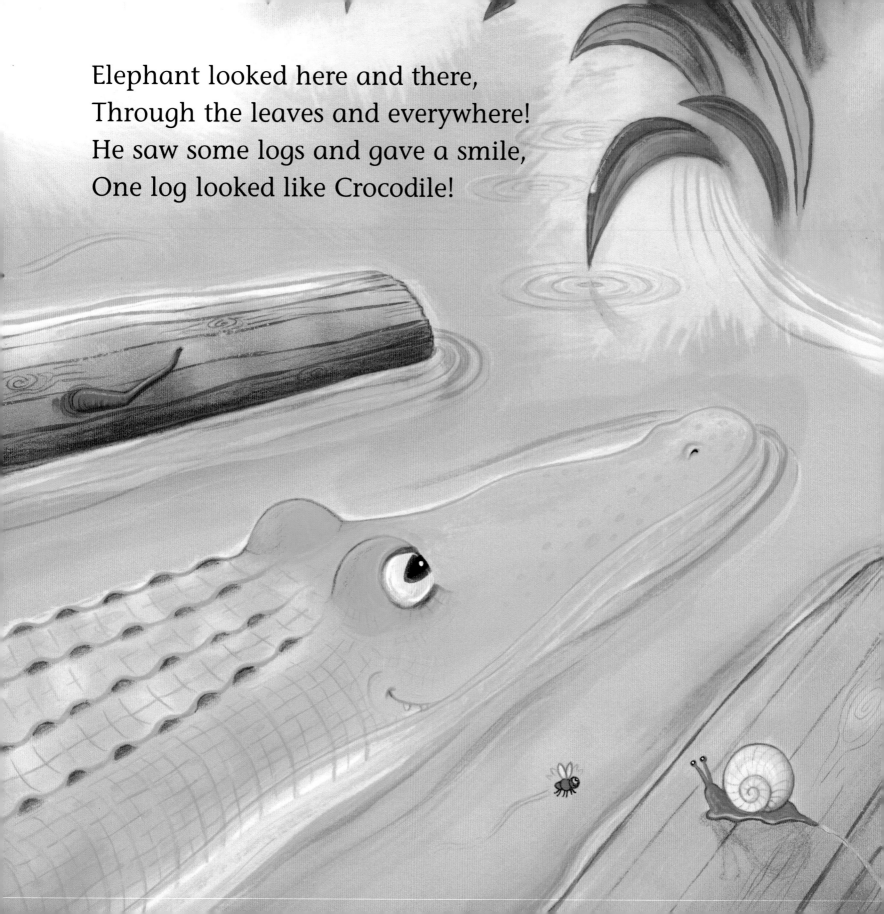

Stick Insect hid on a twig,
When Elephant, who's rather big,
Didn't see him sitting there
And nearly squashed him, unaware!

The game went on, he looked about,
Leopard, Giraffe and Lion came out.
Just one was left. He gave a shout,
"Wherever you are, please come out!"

A little voice said, "I'm up here!"
The creatures saw a shape appear.
Chameleon with his clever skin
Can hide himself in anything!

Did you find him in this book?

Read it again and take a look!

HOW ANIMALS HIDE

It was difficult for Elephant to find his friends during their game of hide-and-seek. This is because each of the jungle animals had a special disguise called **camouflage** to help them hide.

Some animals are the same **color** as the surroundings in which they live, like the tawny-colored Lion who spends most of his time in dry grassy plains, and Parrot who has green feathers to match the color of the leafy treetops. Other creatures have a **pattern** on their coats that helps them blend in to their environment — just like Leopard, whose spots match the patchy sunlight of the jungle, and Giraffe who blends in with the trees and leaves.

Stick Insect and Crocodile's camouflages are a little different, because their **shape** and **texture** can make them appear to be something different — a stick on a jungle floor, or a floating log by the riverside.

All the animal camouflages are good, but not nearly as clever as Chameleon's. He can actually change the color of his skin to match the background into which he chooses to disappear. He can do this because he has clear, scaly skin that has smaller-sized cells of different colors such as yellow, red and brown underneath. To change color, some cells get bigger, and others become smaller, turning Chameleon the color he wants to be.

Did you see all the different colors that Chameleon adopted when he was hiding? See if you can count them. He really is a Clever Chameleon!

For Elizabeth and all my family — A. L.

Barefoot Books, 2067 Massachusetts Ave, Cambridge, MA 02140. Text and illustrations copyright © 2005 by Ali Lodge. The moral right of Ali Lodge to be identified as the author and the illustrator of this work has been asserted. First published in the United States of America in 2005 by Barefoot Books Inc. All rights reserved. No part of this book may be reproduced in any form or by any means, electronic or mechanical, including photocopying, recording or by any information storage and retrieval system, without permission in writing from the publisher.

This book was typeset in Stone Informal. The illustrations were prepared in acrylic paints, watercolor pencil crayons and computer-generated paint effects on Seawhite 220gsm cartridge paper. Graphic design by Jemima Lumley, Bristol. Color separation by Grafiscan, Verona. Printed and bound in China by South China Printing Co. Ltd. This book has been printed on 100% acid-free paper.

Library of Congress Cataloging-in-Publication Data
Lodge, Ali.
  Clever chameleon / written and illustrated by Ali Lodge.
    p. cm.
  Summary: Jungle animals play hide-and-seek to teach children about how animals hide in the wild.
  ISBN 1-84148-347-8 (hardcover : alk. paper) [1. Hide-and-seek--Fiction. 2. Animals--Fiction. 3. Camouflage (Biology)--Fiction. 4. Stories in rhyme.] I. Title.

PZ8.3.L823Cl 2005
[E]--dc22

2004026398

1 3 5 7 9 8 6 4 2

Barefoot Books
Celebrating Art and Story

At Barefoot Books, we celebrate art and story with books that open the hearts and minds of children from all walks of life, inspiring them to read deeper, search further, and explore their own creative gifts. Taking our inspiration from many different cultures, we focus on themes that encourage independence of spirit, enthusiasm for learning, and acceptance of other traditions. Thoughtfully prepared by writers, artists and storytellers from all over the world, our products combine the best of the present with the best of the past to educate our children as the caretakers of tomorrow.

*www.**barefootbooks**.com*